My First
Communion Album

Written by
Rev. Victor Hoagland, C.P.

Illustrated by
Samuel J. Butcher

The Regina Press
New York

Presented to:_____

By:_____

On:_____

My First
Holy Communion

_____ received the
Body and Blood of our Lord Jesus
Christ for the first time

this _____ day of _____

in the year of our Lord _____

Church of _____

_____

_____

_____

Pastor _____

My Relatives

Name	Relationship
_____	_____
_____	_____
_____	_____
_____	_____
_____	_____
_____	_____
_____	_____
_____	_____
_____	_____
_____	_____
_____	_____
_____	_____
_____	_____
_____	_____

My Friends

Name

Name

_____

_____

_____

_____

_____

_____

_____

_____

_____

_____

_____

_____

_____

_____

_____

Gifts

Name	Gift
_____	_____
_____	_____
_____	_____
_____	_____
_____	_____
_____	_____
_____	_____
_____	_____
_____	_____
_____	_____
_____	_____
_____	_____
_____	_____
_____	_____
_____	_____
_____	_____

Prayers & Devotions

The Sign of the Cross

In the name of the Father, and of the Son, and
of the Holy Spirit. Amen.

The Our Father

Our Father, who art in heaven,
hallowed be thy name,
thy kingdom come,
thy will be done,
on earth as it is in heaven.
Give us this day our daily bread,
and forgive us our trespasses
as we forgive those
who trespass against us,
and lead us not into temptation,
but deliver us from evil. Amen.

The Hail Mary

Hail Mary, full of grace,
the Lord is with thee;
blessed art thou among women,
and blessed is the fruit
of thy womb, Jesus.
Holy Mary, Mother of God,
pray for us sinners now
and at the hour of our death. Amen.

Glory Be

Glory be to the Father and to the Son and to the Holy Spirit, as it was in the beginning, is now and ever shall be, world without end. Amen.

Grace Before Meals

Bless us, O Lord, and these your gifts which we are about to receive from your bounty through Christ our Lord. Amen.

Grace After Meals

We give you thanks, O almighty God, for all your benefits; you who live and reign, world without end. Amen.

The Apostles' Creed

I believe in God, the Father almighty, creator of heaven and earth. I believe in Jesus Christ, his only Son, our Lord. He was conceived by the power of the Holy Spirit and born of the Virgin Mary. He suffered under Pontius Pilate, was crucified, died, and was buried. He descended to the dead. On the third day he rose again. He ascended into heaven, and is seated at the right hand of the Father. He will come again to judge the living and the dead. I believe in the Holy Spirit, the holy Catholic Church, the communion of saints, the forgiveness of sins, the resurrection of the body, and the life everlasting. Amen.

The Rosary

The Joyful Mysteries

1. The Coming of Jesus is Announced
2. Mary Visits Elizabeth
3. Jesus is Born
4. Jesus is Presented to God
5. Jesus is Found in the Temple

The Sorrowful Mysteries

1. Jesus' Agony in the Garden
2. Jesus is Whipped
3. Jesus is Crowned with Thorns
4. Jesus Carries His Cross
5. Jesus Dies on the Cross

The Glorious Mysteries

1. Jesus Rises from His Tomb
2. Jesus Ascends to Heaven
3. The Holy Spirit Descends
4. Mary is Assumed into Heaven
5. Mary is Crowned in Heaven

The prayers of the Rosary are The Sign of the Cross, The Glory Be, The Our Father, the Hail Mary and the Apostles' Creed.

The Ten Commandments

1. I, the Lord, am your God. You shall not have other gods besides me.

2. You shall not take the name of the Lord, your God, in vain.

3. Remember to keep holy the sabbath day.

4. Honor your father and your mother.

5. You shall not kill.

6. You shall not commit adultery.

7. You shall not steal.

8. You shall not bear false witness against your neighbor.

9. You shall not covet your neighbor's wife.

10. You shall not covet anything that belongs to your neighbor.

The Beatitudes

1. Blessed are the poor in spirit, for the kingdom of heaven is theirs.

2. Blessed are those who are sad, for they shall be comforted.

3. Blessed are the mild and gentle, for they shall inherit the land.

4. Blessed are those who hunger and thirst for justice, for they shall be filled.

5. Blessed are the merciful, for they shall receive mercy.

6. Blessed are the pure in heart, for they shall see God.

7. Blessed are those who make peace, for they shall be called the children of God.

8. Blessed are those who suffer for my sake, for heaven will be theirs.

My Pictures